THE BABY THAT ROARED!

Simon Puttock

illustrated by

Nadia Shireen

nosy
Crow

For my family
S.P.

Inspired by the energy, wit and
sartorial styling of Dr Harris Ahmed
N.S.

First published 2012 by Nosy Crow Ltd
The Crow's Nest, 10a Lant Street,
London SE1 1QR
www.nosycrow.com

This edition published 2015
ISBN 978 0 85763 654 6

Nosy Crow and associated logos are trademarks
and/or registered trademarks of Nosy Crow Ltd

Text copyright © Simon Puttock 2012
Illustrations copyright © Nadia Shireen 2012

The right of Simon Puttock to be identified as the author
and Nadia Shireen to be identified as the illustrator of
this work has been asserted

A CIP catalogue record for this book is available
from the British Library.

Printed in China by Imago

1 3 5 7 9 8 6 4 2

Mr and Mrs Deer had **no baby**
of their own to **love** and to **cuddle**
and to **read a story** to . . .

– but, oh! –

how they wished that they had.

Then one day,

they found a bundle on the doorstep.

The bundle had a note attached,

which said . . .

Then she popped it into the laundry basket, which was just the right size
for a bed. But, no sooner had she put the baby down,
than it let out a great big

ROAR!

"I expect it's hungry," said Mr Deer. "Babies usually are."

But the baby didn't want
cheese

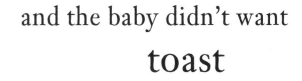

and the baby didn't want
toast

and the baby
didn't want
cabbages

or **cucumbers**

or **cauliflowers!**

What **did** the baby **want** to eat?

"We must get **Uncle Duncan**," said Mrs Deer. "He's bound to know."

"A baby?"
said Uncle Duncan.

"A dear little baby?
I shall come at once!"

"Babies need milk," said Uncle Duncan. "You must warm some up immediately."

But . . .

. . . when Mr and Mrs Deer came back — how very **peculiar!**
Uncle Duncan had disappeared, and the baby was **still**

ROARING!

"**Phew,**" said Mrs Deer,
with a sniff.
"What's that terrible **smell?**"

"**Ew!**" said Mr Deer. "I think this baby needs
changing. We must ask Auntie Agnes —
she generally knows what's what."

"**Nappies!**" said Auntie Agnes.
"And clean towels and special
ointment too!
Now run along and fetch them,
quick as you can."

But . . .

. . . when Mr and Mrs Deer came back – how very **peculiar!** Auntie Agnes had disappeared, and the baby was still **roaring!**

"Oh, poor little baby,"
said Mr Deer.
"Whatever shall we do?"

"Perhaps," said Mrs Deer, "it isn't feeling very well? We must call Doctor Fox to come and take a look."

ROAR!

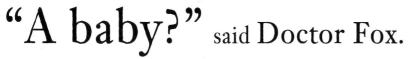

"A baby?" said Doctor Fox.

"A dear little baby?

I shall come at once!"

"I shall need **peace** and **quiet** to examine this baby," said Doctor Fox.

"Now run along you two
and leave everything to me."

Mr and Mrs Deer ran along
and waited and waited
and waited.

ROAR!
ROAR!
ROAR!

But the baby went on roaring.
They had to know
what was happening,
so they tiptoed in and . . .

. . . how very **peculiar!**
Doctor Fox had disappeared,
and the baby was still

ROARING!

"Oh no!" said Mrs Deer.
"What shall we do now?"

"Granny Bear,"
said Mr Deer,
"will know exactly
what to do."

Granny Bear came at once.
She took one look at the poor little,
dear little, roaring, **roaring**
baby and said,

"I know **exactly** what to do.
This baby needs a **burping**."

And she picked up the
baby and patted it.

And **patted** it

and **patted** it,

until . . .

It was really very **peculiar!**

Out came
Uncle Duncan

and out came
Auntie Agnes

and out came
Doctor Fox, too!
And none of them looked the
least bit pleased.

"That's not a dear little baby!"
cried Granny Bear.

"That is a LITTLE

ROAR!

And it was, too!
And it took to its heels and away it ran,

and they never,
ever, ever saw it again.

As for **Mr** and **Mrs Deer**, well. . . .

. . . they found themselves . . .

. . . a sweet little **kitten** to **love** instead!